Ernest the Heroic Lion-tamer

Damon Burnard

Young Lions

First published in Great Britain by
A & C Black (Publishers) Ltd 1993
First published in Young Lions 1994

Young Lions is an imprint of the Children's Division
part of HarperCollins Publishers Ltd.
77/85 Fulham Palace Road, London W6 8JB

ISBN 0-00-674811-2

Printed and bound in Great Britain by HarperCollins Manufacturing, Glasgow

They'd gulped at the fire-eater feasting on her flaming fare!

They'd split their sides laughing at the clowns' crazy capers!

'And now,' Tobias Toast announced,

Into the ring stepped Ernest. His
spangled uniform sparkled in the
spotlight and the plume on his hat
stood tall and proud.

Then into the ring leapt . . .

. . . a LION!

He let out a series of blood-curdling
roars . . .

. . . and slashed at the air
with his awesome claws!

The lion's name was Brian.
Brian Lion.

Ernest the Heroic Lion-tamer
stood his ground.

Brian Lion opened
his jaws
WIDE.

Scary, isn't he?

Reader's voice

Phew! Scarier
than a mutant,
man-eating
spider, I
reckon!

In that case, before we go any
further, there's something you
should know.

Chapter Two

Brian Lion was, in fact,
a very sensible lion.

He loved to eat Italian food and
enjoyed reading books by Charles
Dickens – even the really long ones
which weigh a ton.

Norman, the Circus Strong-man,
during his attempt to lift the
complete works of Charles Dickens.
His attempt failed.

Brian Lion had shared a caravan with Ernest since 1973. That was the year they began travelling with the circus and performing their act.

So you see, eating Ernest was the last thing on Brian Lion's mind!

But the crowd didn't know this.

They sat in silence
as the drums rolled.

They saw Brian open his jaws wide.

They saw the saliva dribbling down
his terrifying teeth!

They saw Ernest climb a step-ladder . . .

. . . and stick his head into Brian Lion's mouth!

Not a soul stirred.

except me!

And then . . .

Chapter Three

In the time it took Ernest to remove
his head from Brian Lion's mouth,
the Big Top had emptied.

The whole audience had gone home, back to their televisions and videos, to watch . . . violence . . . romance . . . stupidity . . . and lies.

Anything. Anything at all. Just so long as it wasn't a man wearing a silly hat, sticking his head into a lion's mouth!

Chapter Four

Ernest asked as the other
performers gathered round.

said the trapeze artistes.

said the fire-eater.

said the human cannon-ball.

said the clowns.

Tobias Toast placed a hand on the
Heroic Lion-tamer's shoulder.

This was not the first time the
audience had left during Ernest's
act. Tobias Toast had watched it
happen every night for months.

23

But today is Tuesday! That only leaves me.. umm...err...um....

FOUR MORE NIGHTS!

That's right! You subtract very well! Have you ever thought about a career in accountancy?

wheeze!

Goodnight, Ernest. And good luck!

Ha ha ha! Those sneaky clowns! They're always switching my cigars for joke ones! Ha ha...

KER-BLAM!

Ha.

Grrrr...

Chapter Five

Slowly Ernest made his way back
to the caravan he shared with
Brian Lion.

His sorry head sank so low,
a nearby elephant trumpeted,

Whenever he was sad or depressed, Ernest became a very rude and grumpy Heroic Lion-tamer.

Since the act had been going so badly, he was grumpy and rude nearly all the time.
(See diagram over page.)

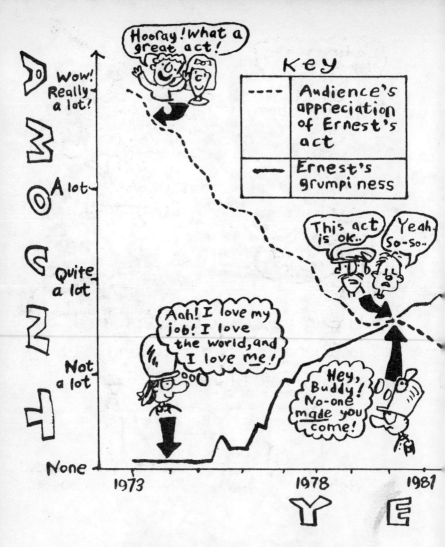

The black line on this handy chart shows what's happened to Ernest's grumpiness over the years. The dotted line shows what's happened to the audience's appreciation of

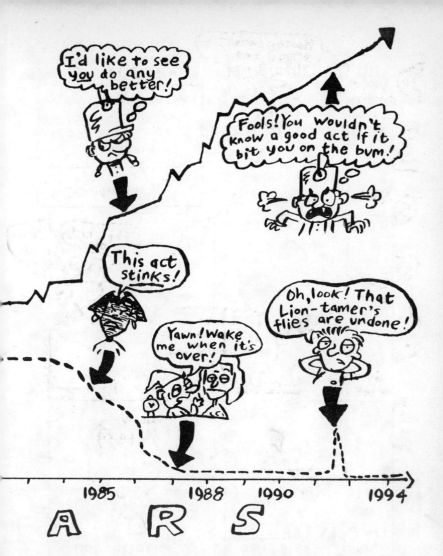

Ernest's act over the same period.
As you can see, the less the
audience liked the act, the grumpier
and ruder Ernest became.

And who do you think bore the brunt of Ernest's foul moods? (Answer at bottom of page.)

Was it . . .

1: Norman, the circus strong-man?

2: Sheila, the performing seal?

3: Colin, the opera-singing mouse? Or....

4: Brian Lion?

ANSWER: Yes, you guessed it. Brian Lion, that's who.

30

Chapter Six

Ernest had become so grumpy, the only time he spoke to Brian Lion nowadays was to grumble at him, or order him about. Often he'd do BOTH. He'd say things like:

and . . .

Microscopic cake crumbs

or . . .

Pouf up the plume in my hat! Remember, if it wasn't for me, you'd be stuck in a zoo!

Reader's voice

Oh boy! He's got a nerve, talking to Brian Lion that way!

A nerve? Actually, I've got _millions_ of nerves, you silly little reader!

Cripes! He _is_ rude, isn't he? What did Brian Lion do about it? Did he stand on Ernest's chest until he apologised?

Go on, say it: "I'm sorry."

Gnnn....!

No, he didn't.

No, he didn't.

He did exactly what
he was told.

If you'll just stop talking for one
second, I'll explain.

You see, Brian Lion could still remember the old days, when things were different; a time when he and Ernest had barrels of fun.

a) The Old Days   b) Nowadays

Brian Lion knew that Ernest was miserable because the act was going badly. Indeed, more than once he'd spied Ernest talking to himself in front of the bathroom mirror.

Poor Ernest! He's eating himself up inside!

And so Brian put up with the moods and did as he was told, because he hoped it would make Ernest cheerful again.

Oh, I see. Still, if I was Brian, I'd have chased Ernest around the ring, until...

Reader's voice-again!

Reader?

Yes?

Please try not to interrupt so much!

Whoops! I'm sorry! I promise it won't happen again!

Thank you.

Yeah! Put a sock in it, Motor-mouth!

Chapter Seven

When Ernest returned to the caravan that night, he was very depressed. He drank a bottle of flat cola and lay, face down, on the kitchen floor.

Hey, Ernie! What did Tobias want to talk to you about?

Mind your own business. What's for dinner?

It took Brian Lion every ounce of self-control to keep his temper.

Chapter Eight

For the next three nights, Ernest the Heroic Lion-tamer tried his best to spice up the act.

WEDNESDAY

THURSDAY

FRIDAY

Ernest got grumpier . . .

and grumpier . . .

and grumpier . . .

'Why do you keep changing the act?' asked Brian Lion. 'No reason,' Ernest lied.

Chapter Nine

It was Saturday Night; Ernest's very last chance. As he and Brian Lion waited their turn backstage, Ernest was in a record-breaking bad mood.

(The previous record was set by Charity Makepeace Smithereen, a Victorian schoolgirl.

Protesting against her parent's demand that she finish her greens, she held her breath from December 19th 1879 until January 14th 1880, whereupon she exploded.)

Ernest the Heroic Lion-tamer
hadn't an idea left in his brain.

He was terribly depressed. He
snapped and snarled at poor Brian
without pausing for breath.

At last the clowns finished their act.
'And now,' Tobias Toast
announced,

Ernest's spangled suit sparkled in
the spotlight as he stepped into
the ring.

But the plume on his
hat was all droopy,
and his tummy
was full of
butterflies.

Into the ring leapt Brian Lion.

He opened wide his
fearsome jaws.

Gloomily Ernest stuck
his head inside.

47

Tobias Toast started to tear up
Ernest's contract.

The crowd fell silent.

Ernest felt terrible.

'It's all over! I know it!' he thought. 'It's just a matter of seconds until they start to yawn!' There was nothing left for Ernest to do except take it out on Brian Lion. As usual.

That was the last straw.

Sirens wailed inside Brian's head.

Bells clanged . . .

buttons were pressed . . .

steam shot out of his ears.

With one toss of his great golden
head, he swallowed Ernest up.

Whole.

Chapter Ten

No one yawned.
No one moved
a muscle.

A tiny voice rose up
from Brian Lion's
stomach.

Help!
Let me
out!

'Only if you promise to stop being such a beast!' said Brian.

Brian Lion took a deep breath . . .

55

Ernest flew high into the air and landed with a bump on his bottom.

Chapter Eleven

The audience were going crazy.

They'd never seen a lion swallow a lion-tamer before, let alone spit him out again in one piece!

Together Ernest and Brian
bowed graciously to
thunderous applause.

The other acts gathered round in
excitement.

said the fire-eater.

said the human
cannon-ball.

said the trapeze artistes.

said the clowns.

said Tobias Toast.

This new act is going to make me — I mean, us three — very rich and famous! Cough!

Wheeze! Here, take these! Splutter!

He handed Brian and Ernest a new contract AND a voucher for a meal for two at a nearby Italian restaurant.

Chapter Twelve